Waste Not

And Other Funny Zombie Stories

Rhonda Parrish

Poise and Pen Publishing

www.rhondaparrish.com
www.poiseandpen.com

Publisher's Note: This is a work of fiction. Names, characters, places, and incidents are a product of the author's imagination. Locales and public names are sometimes used for atmospheric purposes. Any resemblance to actual people, living or dead, or to businesses, companies, events, institutions, or locales is completely coincidental.

Book Layout ©2017 BookDesignTemplates.com

Cover Design by James, GoOnWrite.com

Waste Not/ Rhonda Parrish. -- 1st ed.
ISBN 978-0993699009

Contents

Waste Not

The sun peeked over the horizon, sending its golden light out over the land. The beams danced on the water in the creek and flowed over the green field of corn. Even through the dirty hayloft window it was a beautiful sight, a lovely moment. Then he had to go and spoil it.

"You still in bed? Useless as yer pa! Git up. Those pigs won't feed 'imselves." Grandpa's voice, slurred already, drowned out the morning birdsong.

I rolled out of bed and got dressed, then wandered into the kitchen-area. He could scream all he wanted, I wasn't going to run for him. If he was in such a hurry for the pigs to get fed he could do it his own damned self for a change.

He sat at the scarred table that I'm told had been in the family for generations. All's I know for sure is that it's heavy as sin. Damned thing had been a bitch to get into the hayloft when we'd moved out of the house to get off the ground level. I glanced in his direction and confirmed, as if there were any doubt, that he was drunk. It was there, in his liquid posture and glassy eyes. He'd always been a drunk, but it got worse after the ghouls came, and worse again a couple years back when he drank the county dry and had to start brewing his own poison.

I grabbed a couple cold biscuits out of the basket on the table and jammed them into the pocket of my overalls. Gran's back was to me, but she turned as I put my arm around her shoulder, planting a kiss on her soft, wrinkled cheek. "Good morning."

"Morning," she said, her voice low so as not to draw Grandpa's attention. He hadn't done it recently, not since I told him anything he did to Gran I'd do back to him, but he used to hit her. A lot. "I'll collect the eggs shortly, but do you mind milking the cow? My knees aren't what they once were."

"Of course." I smiled at Gran, and after giving her shoulder one last squeeze climbed down the ladder into the barn proper.

I milked Clarabelle, then let her out into the field with her calf and our two heifers. I'd been separating her from the calf at night to start the weaning process and ensure some milk for us. I was just shutting the big door when Grandpa came down. He grumbled at me, nothing new, and then stumbled out the big door and into the field. I halfway-hoped he'd get into the bull's field. Bataar had never been a friendly bull and having his field made so much smaller hadn't improved his temperament. There wasn't much I could do about it though. I had to keep everything of value, including him, inside the perimeter. I was the only one who could maintain it so the chain link fence I used to pen us in, and the ghouls out, only enclosed a fraction of the original farm.

Originally, the fence had been electrified, but power had run out long ago. Truth-be-told, I was halfway happy when it did. On my daily patrols round the fence line I found a lot more fried birds and bunnies than I did ghouls. Living out in the middle of nowhere had its perks. Less people meant less ghouls. I hadn't even seen sign of one in weeks.

I was just finishing with the pigs when I heard him holler. I drew my pistol, not so complacent I'd stopped carrying it, and ran toward the sound. My boots sounded hollow against the hard-packed earth around the corrals as I ran toward the shell of the old farmhouse. The ghoul, a fetid, long-dead thing with barely enough of itself left to stand, held Grandpa up against the boarded-up picture window. The old drunk's screams were constant, but rose in pitch as he saw me. Then, the ghoul buried its face in his throat and the scream bubbled away into a wet gurgling sound. I was too late.

I shot the ghoul in the back of its head. The black and green sludge which had replaced the creature's blood and brain as it decomposed splattered Grandpa's face and the house. The ghoul fell with a soft thud at Grandpa's feet. He, too, slumped to the ground, clutching the bleeding wound in his throat, his mouth gasping like a landed fish. His eyes were wide with awareness of his fate. The scent of the ghoul reached my nostrils and I retched, then lifted my gun once more.

"Don't!" Gran's voice stopped me as she hobbled over from the barn.

"He's been bit, Gran, I'm sorry."

I looked back at Grandpa. He was shaking his head from side to side, like a dog with a tug-rope, and trying to stand. Blood loss and alcohol kept him from success. Still, as pitiful as he looked I had no sympathy for him. Not even a little.

"I know," she nodded, "but I have an idea. Waste not, want not."

Grandpa had grown up during the depression and 'waste not, want not' was one of his favourite things to say. Over and over. When the ghouls had gotten my Pa, Grandpa had insisted on stripping him naked before burying him, to save the clothes. "He won't need 'em where he's going," he'd said. "Waste not, want not."

Gran's a clever lady, and by working quickly, before Grandpa bled out and turned we managed to put her plan into action. He's up there now, thrashing and failing, but the way I impaled him there's no way he's getting loose until his ribcage rots. By then he won't be a danger to anyone, and in the meantime you've never seen a more effective scarecrow.

Feeders

The last time I saw my former feeder he was rushing out the door to work. I thought it odd when he didn't come home that night, but truthfully, I welcomed his absence. It meant I didn't have to endure his incessant ruffling of my fur, or the condescending high-pitched voice he reserved exclusively for talking to me. Plus, I got to stretch out and take up all the bed I wanted.

The next morning I was woken by the sound of a loud explosion. It hurt my ears and rattled the house's windows. After a nice, long stretch, I had a bite to eat and climbed into the west-facing window upstairs. Smoke filled the air and irritated my nose. It must have been even worse on the other side of the glass.

Over the next few days smoke came and went, some clouds more offensive than others. Mostly I stayed in my window, enjoying the sun on my fur and the interesting view below. Ghouls chased the feeders through the streets. They came in waves, like the fires. One group of ghouls and feeders would pass through with much screaming, banging and excitement, and then, sometimes for hours at a time, the world would be silent. Eerily silent. Even those insufferably chirpy birds had nothing to say. Then, eventually, inevitably, another wave of predator and prey would pass by, giving me something to watch and leaving carnage in their wake.

It was a good life.

Then my water dish ran dry.

That was my first hint something had gone wrong.

Happily, my feeder wasn't much of a handyman and so the tap in the kitchen sink always dripped. That meant I didn't go thirsty, but it was pretty tedious having to get my water drop by drop rather than by lapping it from a dish. At least it was fresh, I guess, but still--

My food dish was the next casualty.

I knew where my feeder kept the food, so it was only a matter of outsmarting the cupboard door to get it open. I managed that in no time at all, and sliced the side of the bag open faster than you can say Eukanuba. I had a hell of a feast. A little too big of one, as it turned out. I left a couple piles of barf in the living room, and without a feeder around to clean them up, they began to smell. Happily, they eventually dried up and the smell went away, but I still had to *look* at them.

They weren't the only nasty things either. My litter box was unbelievable. After only a few nights it was not a pleasant place to visit and eventually there was no point in trying to bury anything in there. At some point I gave up and began going *near* the litter box rather than in it.

And then things started to get bad.

I was out of food, out of places to do my business and I was spending most of my day trying to fill up on the water that dripped from the tap rather than watching the goings on outside. And the events outside were quite interesting.

While the ghouls physical bodies had stayed in the same condition over time, their wounds neither healing nor their flesh rotting, their clothing had deteriorated. I could tell how fresh they were by what they wore. The newest ones still had clothes on; blood-stained and dirty, but whole. Most of them, though, were clad in filthy things that looked more like rags than actual clothes and the oldest ghouls were naked but for the layers of blood and dirt that clung to them like bodypaint.

What was even more remarkable was how they moved. When they'd first started appearing on my street, the ghouls had wandered aimlessly, pinballing off one another unless they scented or sensed a feeder. Then they would shuffle after them, groaning. Now they seemed to have found a purpose. They moved deliberately. Slowly, but with far more control and finesse than before and when they were in pursuit of a feeder they chased them quicker, and quieter.

However, as interesting as all that was, it wasn't going to get my littler box cleaned or my food dish filled. Things were becoming desperate. Obviously I had to leave the house, at least for long enough to find some loose dirt and hunt up some food, but my feeder hadn't left any doors or windows open when he left for work.

So I got to work on the walls.

Once, when I was young, I'd decided to sharpen my claws on them. My feeder had been plenty grumpy but I'd learned an important thing: claws can cut through drywall.

It was difficult work, work I wasn't at all suited for. It dulled my claws and I got covered in dusty, itchy detritus. What's more, it required a lot of time. I took several naps in between when I started and when the first glimmer of daylight shone through the hole I'd scratched out, and I was plenty hungry. It was two naps more before the hole was big enough for me to squeeze myself through. In retrospect it's probably a good thing I'd lost a little weight while I was holed up in the house without my feeder, or I would have had to expend even *more* effort.

I hadn't been out of the house since I'd been a kitten. It was weird, but pretty awesome. The grass felt cool and soft under my sore paws, the sun was warm on my back, and the air (now that the fires had died down) was fresh and sweet. I rolled around in the grass, even tasted some of it, and was off to find a soft patch of dirt to do my business in, when he spotted me. A feeder.

"A cat!" he called in a stage whisper, pointing at me from around the corner of the neighbor's house.

I looked him over. He didn't look much cleaner than the ghouls. His clothes hung from him as though they'd been made for someone far larger, his eyes were sunken and his skin grey. In fact, I'm not sure how I knew he was a feeder and not a ghoul. It must have been the gleam of life in his eyes. Eyes that were pointed right at me, looking at me in a way no feeder ever had before -- with hunger.

She saved me. The ghoul.

She was the size of my former feeder's niece. She'd be big enough to open doors, back in the day, but not to reach my treats on the back of the kitchen counter without a stool. Her hair had been blonde, but was now a muddy mix of colors. It was still pulled into pigtails, but

while they may once have been perky and taut, now they drooped and
were skewed to the sides.

The feeder was climbing over the fence toward me, hunger in his
eyes. A woman waited on the other side of the fence, her fingers
curled through the chain link, her mouth open, gaping dumbly.

I turned to run, but was saved the effort when the ghoul stepped in
between myself and the feeder. She'd been in the bushes. I hadn't seen
or smelled her there, and neither did the feeder. When she stepped
between the two of us he reeled backward, falling onto his bottom. He
scrambled to get his feet back under him while the woman screamed
at him from the other side of the fence. The ghoul just stood there,
between us, watching him.

I followed her after that. Eventually she went to a battered
warehouse, several blocks away. They were long blocks for my short
legs, especially food-deprived as I was, but I'm not so foolish as to
give up a keeper when I find one. So the warehouse is home now.

We're not alone here, there are dozens of other ghouls who come
and go at random times. It's not as warm as my other house was and
the windows are grimy, but some of them face west so I can enjoy the
sunlight for most of the day, and the feeders tend to stay away because
they are afraid of the ghouls which keeps them from trying to put me
in their bellies.

I haven't a taste for mice, and birds are clever little things that
require stealth and patience to slay. I have little of either. I watch
others of my kind from the window, they skulk in shadows, growing
thin and weak, but not me. She brings me food. Hunks of meat, red
and dripping, pieces of bruise-black liver, or bones with skin and
muscles still attached. I lick the sanguine drops from her fingers and
tangle myself around her legs to show my gratitude.

It's a different life than the one I had before, but it's a good one.
Best of all, I don't have to endure her mussing up my fur with her
attentions, or talking to me in that condescending tone feeders reserve
just for my kind.

...Oh My!

Kaj hummed the tune to The Lollypop Guild as he skipped toward home. He executed a hop-turn and stumbled. "It's the light," he told himself, though he knew it to be a lie. The problem, as evidenced by the fact even the tip of his nose was numb, was all the wine he'd consumed at Boj's party. His excess was forgivable though, it wasn't everyday a house dropped out of the sky and squished the Wicked Witch of the East.

Remembering the look on her face as the shadow of the house pinned her in place made him laugh and his giggle ended in a hiccup as he rounded the corner of the tall hedge that circled the town center.

There it was, in the center of town square. The house. Its landing hadn't done it any favors, it leaned to one side and detritus littered the ground around it. Everything had been left where it fell in order to celebrate the witch's death but later today they'd have to figure out what to do with it. They couldn't just leave it; there was the body of a witch under there somewhere.

Kaj peered at it through bloodshot eyes. Houses in Kansas were different than those of Munchkinland. They were bigger, for one thing, and not nearly as colorful. The glass had shattered on impact and the pieces that crunched under his boots as he stepped closer were clear, not tinted every shade of the rainbow like the windows of his own home.

He leaned against the side of the building and stood on his tip toes to peer in a window. Inside, things had been tossed this way and that which made sense since Dorothy said she'd been caught in a twisting wind that wound the house up more than a top.

A scraping sound broke the near silence of the morning and Kaj jumped and looked around. The little flutter of guilt and nerves in his stomach made him laugh at himself. No one else was about, they were all at home asleep or else back at Boj's enjoying the last of the drink.

Stepping away from the house he dusted his hands off on his dark blue trousers and turned in the direction of home. He'd reached the bushes on the other side of the square when he heard it again. A soft scraping sound coming from Dorothy's house. Kaj paused, tilted his head and cupped his ear to hear the noise better if it repeated. It did.

He frowned. His imagination immediately going to all the stories about the Wicked Witch of the East from his childhood. Stories about the evil magic she used, the power she had over life and death. His thoughts lingered on the one recurring theme from those stories—only one thing could kill the witch. What if that one thing wasn't actually a house falling from the sky? What if she hadn't died after all? What if she was under there trying to claw her way out? But she couldn't be alive, could she? Dorothy had taken her slippers off and that couldn't happen while the witch still breathed and he'd seen with his very own eyes how her feet curled up and withered beneath the house.

The noise came again. A scratching, scraping noise that was becoming louder, louder and more persistent. If it wasn't the witch, someone or something else was in there. It's just a rat, he told himself, but his feet didn't obey his halfhearted command to keep walking home.

"Hullo?" he called, surprised to hear how weak his voice sounded, how thin. The sound came again and this time he thought he saw, through the window, some of the shadows inside shift. "Hullo?"

"Hullo!" a voice behind him said cheerily.

Kaj jumped, swallowing the scream that had flown up into his throat, and spun around to find Mooki smiling at him. "Gah! I—that is, you startled me."

"Well," Mooki said, "you did say hullo."

Mooki's face was flushed and his eyes glassy. Kaj had seen him at Boj's party and could guess the cause for both. Realizing that he was the more sober of the two made Kaj smile and, for some reason increased his confidence. He straightened his shoulders and nodded toward Dorothy's house. "I thought I saw something in there."

"In the house?" Mooki leaned forward dramatically, his eyes narrowed as he squinted at the building.

"Yes, there was a sound—there. That's it. Did you hear that?"

Mooki's eyes widened and he nodded. "I did! What do you suppose it is?"

"I don't know," Kaj answered then raised an eyebrow. "Why don't you go find out?"

"Okay," Mooki shrugged and took a crooked step toward the door. Kaj grabbed his sleeve to pull him back, and Mooki stumbled and turned nearly full circle in order to regain his balance. When he recovered his footing he squinted at Kaj. "Whaddjya do that for?"

"What if it's the witch?"

"If it's the witch we have big problems. She's dead." Mooki laughed and started walking back toward the house. "It's probably a cat."

The sound came again, a ripping noise, like wood being splintered, and Mooki paused but then continued. Kaj let him go.

Kaj took a seat by the bushes and watched as Mooki opened the door and stood in the opening. He looked bizarrely out of proportion, the doorknob was almost taller than he was.

"Hullo?" Mooki called, then he stepped into the house.

Moments later, Mooki's scream preceded him out the door. He didn't run out, he fell. His legs were still in the house while his upper body stuck out the door. Even across the distance that separated them Kaj could see his friend's face, mutated by terror. Mooki was scrambling, arms flailing wildly as he dragged himself out the door.

Kaj stumbled toward Mooki as his screams reached a pitch higher than Kaj had ever heard before. Mooki dragged his lower body from the house just as Kaj came within spitting distance. His legs were a bloody mess. Kaj was stunned, he'd never seen an injury like that before and no idea idea what could cause it. Mookie crawled a short distance away and then collapsed onto the ground. Great waves of blood gushed out of his thigh with regularity Kaj immediately identified as his heartbeat.

Kaj ran toward his friend, pressing his palms against the throbbing wound. As Mooki's life gushed out of him, Kaj knew there was nothing he could do. "Oh Mooki! What happened to you?" he cried.

Mooki was beyond answering. His eyelids fluttered and he fell limp in Kaj's arms.

Lifting tear-filled eyes, Kaj realized he and Mooki were not alone. The Wicked Witch of the East had followed Mooki out of the house. The stories about her being cursed must have been true! She looked worse than Mooki. She'd been squished nearly flat, all the parts of her body shifted, flattened or exploded by the pressure. She didn't look like she could stand, and she didn't try. She should have been dead, and yet, there she was, crawling across the bricks toward them, her eyes burning with hunger.

Kaj stumbled to his feet and scrambled back from Mooki and the witch. The witche's gaze was attracted to the motion, her head turned and her eyes focused on him. Then, to make things worse, Mooki, poor dead Mooki, sat up beside her. The look on his face wasn't peaceful or even pained, it was feral.

"Help!" he screamed. "Oh please, help!"

The strongest and bravest munchkin Kaj knew was Oko and he was back at Boj's party.

Mooki struggled to his feet and lurched toward him. Kaj jumped away, tripping over some bushes and landing, sprawled painfully on the pavement. Mooki waded through the bushes toward him, his face contorted into a snarl, his fingers curled into claws. He reached toward him and Kaj let him draw near and then kicked him in the chest with both feet. Mooki staggered back, and landed in the bushes.

While Mooki flailed wildly, trying to regain his footing, Kaj jumped to his feet and raced back toward the party.

The party was almost finished. By the time he arrived there were munchkins passed out all over Boj's front lawn. The music had been turned down to a dull murmur and he couldn't see anyone up and moving around. A glance back over his shoulder showed no sign of the witch, but Mooki was not far behind.

"Wake up! Everyone wake up!"

No one stirred. He ran over to the first munchkin he saw, and gave them a shake. "Wake up! They're coming!" The munchkin, who he could now see was Boj didn't respond. His eyes fluttered slightly but when Kaj let him go he slumped back to the ground with all the spirit of a sack of potatoes.

"Oko! Oko, where are you?" Kaj raced across the yard dodging sleeping munchkins, empty glasses, bottles and plates and ran into the house. "Oko!"

Then Boj screamed and Kaj felt tears prick at the back of his eyelids. It was his fault, he'd led them here, but all he'd wanted was to find help to find Oko. Outside, another munchkin, a girl, screamed.

"Oko!"

"What is it?" Relief flooded through him as a familiar voice came from upstairs.

"Oko! We need to help," another scream sounded outside, and then another. Soon there was a chorus of them and Kaj hoped they were caused by munchkins waking up to find out what was happening rather than being attacked.

Oko came down to the landing. He wasn't wearing anything except for his trousers and suspenders. His hair was mussed and his cherubic face pale. Kaj suspected he was beginning to feel his hangover, but no matter how poorly he felt now, he was about to feel a whole lot worse.

There was a small, round window on the landing that looked out over the front lawn. Without a word he pointed at it, and Oko looked out. Oko swore under his breath and then became a juggernaut. He raced to the door, and where Kaj's shouts hadn't managed to rouse anyone, Oko's was. "Everyone," he hollered from the doorway. "Get into the house. Right now. Everyone. In the house. Now!"

From his spot by the window Kaj could see all the munchkins running and stumbling into the house. All the munchkins but Salli, Mooki and Boj. Salli and Mooki were too busy chewing on Boj's arm while he screamed and struggled against them. When Boj's screams ended, about the time all the other munchkins made it into his house Kaj watched him make the same transformation Mooki had. His face went slack and his eyes filled with pure hunger. Tearing himself from the window Kaj went to work boarding up all the ground floor windows.

"I think we're ready for them.," Oko said as they boarded up the last window. "All the windows are shut and they aren't coming through that door easily." He gestured with his head toward the large chest of drawers pushed up against the front door. "What is going on?"

"I don't know," Kaj answered truthfully. He told Oko what had happened, alternating his attention between him and the window. "It's like they were dead but now they aren't," he concluded.

Behind him, munchkins sobbed and murmured amongst themselves. It was as though they were afraid to raise their voices lest the creatures in the yard hear them.

"Could be all those stories about her were true," Oko suggested.

"Could be. Or maybe she cast a spell? Whatever it is, it's not good. The witch was dead. The coroner said so. She was most sincerely dead, but she's not now."

"Where is she?"

"I don't know. She can't stand up, maybe she's still crawling this way."

"Or the other way."

Kaj felt ill, and he didn't think it was all due to his emerging hangover. In fact, now that Oko had planted the thought in his mind, he could almost swear he heard screams coming from the other side of Munchkinville.

A dull banging sound startled everyone in the house and there was a chorus of shrieks, cut short and smothered as reply. Kaj looked out the window to see Mooki pawing at the doorway. He'd apparently forgotten how doorknobs worked, and was sliding his limp hand over the wood, futilely attempting to gain entrance. Salli was beside him, making the same inept petting motions on the wall. Boj struggled to stand behind them.

"They won't get in," Kaj said, looking back at Oko then at the cluster of a half dozen munchkins in the living room. "At least not yet, but the witch is out there somewhere, along with most of the town."

"You're right. We need to get out of here. We need to gather up all the munchkins we can, and go somewhere safer. Somewhere with supplies."

"Town hall." Kaj said. Glancing back out the window at the once familiar faces, now slack and bloodied, he felt guilt stab into his gut. He'd led them here. "You take everyone to town hall and I will go to the Emerald City."

"Emerald City?"

"That's where Glinda is. She's a powerful good witch. She's our only hope against this black magic. With her help maybe we could make these munchkins stay dead. Plus, the wizard needs to be told about this."

"Okay, but be careful. There might be more cannibalistic munchkins out there than we know about."

"I will."

Oko looked at the little group huddled in the living room and then at Kaj. "Okay everyone," he said, raising his voice to cut through their fearful murmurings. "We're going to town hall. We'll go out a back window while these guys are busy up here."

Oko herded the group to a large back window, opened it and slipped out himself to show them that it was safe and easy while Kaj took up the rear and coaxed and encouraged each munchkin in turn until they got out. Finally, when no one was left in the house but himself, Kaj climbed through and dropped the short distance to the ground just in time to hear the last of Oko's instructions. "...go door to door and get people, then bring them and all the food you can carry to the town hall. Move quickly and be careful. We don't know how many more of them there are."

Kaj caught Oko's eye over the heads of the other munchkins as they scattered, moving as quietly as possible to avoid being noticed by Mooki and company. He nodded goodbye and started toward town square, taking a circuitous route to avoid the ravenous munchkins in the front yard.

Glinda always said to start at the beginning, and if he was going to go to the Emerald City that meant the yellow brick road.

The sun was hot and blinding. It fed the steadily growing throb inside his head, and made his stomach swirl like the wind Dorothy rode in on. His tongue felt like it was covered by a dirty sock and his feet were heavy. What's more, his bladder was going to explode if he didn't let some of the beer out soon.

Glancing around warily, Kaj stopped at a tree by town square relieve himself. He was just about to unzip when he felt an iron grip on his ankle and looked down to see Gabe, his face shredded as though by sharp fingernails. He pulled away but the other munchkin chomped down on the back of his calf at the same time. Shaking like a decapitated chicken, Kaj managed to free himself from Gabe's clutches and stagger backward. Unfortunately, he left a sizable chunk of his leg in the other munchkin's mouth.

Kaj fell back in the middle of the road and scrambled backward like a crab to put some distance between himself and Gabe. Gabe pulled himself out of the bushes by his arms, dragging himself toward Kaj. His lower body was almost non-existent. Only a mangled mess of meat and bone.

With his heart drumming in his chest, Kaj scooted back further, and then used a bush to pull himself upright. His eyes glued on Gabe, who was making very slow progress toward him, Kaj pulled his handkerchief out of his pocket and wrapped it tightly around his leg to stem the bleeding. His leg was still able to support his weight but it throbbed with every heartbeat.

Kaj glared down at Gabe, who continued to inch his way toward him, flailing his arms and making wet grunting noise, and moved deliberately toward the spiral that was the beginning of the Yellow Brick Road.

"I'm off to see the wizard," he hummed under his breath, an attempt at taking his mind off the hole in his leg. "The wonderful wizard of Oz…"

He walked by farmland. The well-tended fields sectioned out with white plank fences sprawled out around him as far as he could see. Sweat beaded his brow and dampened his neck, but he kept going. It got harder as time went by. The urge to lie down and sleep grew stronger along with the heat of the sun. To make matters worse, as the shock of the undead munchkins and the copious amounts of alcohol he'd consumed the night before left his system, his hangover made an appearance. He could feel the seed of it blossoming in his stomach as nausea and in his skull as a headache. It throbbed in time with the wound in his calf, aching with each beat of his heart.

He was worried about his leg. It wasn't bleeding much but it hurt like nothing he'd ever felt before. Kaj stumbled over a short fence into a field of green corn stalks. Crows flew up at his appearance, their chastising voices burning into his head like a flame through straw. "Be quiet!" he shouted, then immediately regretted it and clutched his ears to muffle the renewed shrieking that surrounded him.

He sat down in the shade between the stalks, to rest for a few moments before continuing, but the image of the cannibalistic munchkins he'd left back at Munchkinville stirred him from the ground before too long. The Emerald City was still a long way away and he had to get there soon; before the munchkins ran out of food or became food themselves.

He was weak and feverish. His mouth tasted like cotton and his stomach felt like a maelstrom. Kaj sat down on the edge of the fence and stuck out his leg. The handkerchief was bloodstained and dried in most places. He untied it from around his leg, but it remained stuck in place.

He grabbed one end of the handkerchief and gritting his teeth, pulled it off. The pain tore through him and he screamed loud enough to startle the crows again and send them flapping off in all directions.

The bite had scabbed over in some places but mostly it was still wet and raw. At its center it oozed yellow liquid that smelled bad enough to turn Kaj's still-queasy stomach. The edges were puffy, swollen and bright red. In fact, he could see a fierce scarlet line making its way up his calf directly from the injury.

"That's not good," he said, and his voice sounded like a hoarse croak to his ears.

"It's really not." Oko's voice came from behind him and startled Kaj so that he fell off the fence post. The air was knocked from his lungs and he lay there, staring up at the empty sky, struggling to pull air into his body. Oko's worried face blocked out the blue of sky and he peered down at him on the ground. "Wow. Didn't mean to startle you. You okay?"

"No," Kaj gasped, expending some of the precious air he'd managed to inhale. Then he closed his eyes and waited for the pounding in his head to subside and his heart to stop racing like a mouse's.

"I thought I'd come, too. Got most everyone in the town center and Rin is taking over there, smart girl that Rin. Anyway, I figured two people going to find Glinda was better then one." Oko paused and then spoke again, his voice holding an obviously forced casualness, "Your leg, it don't look good."

"Doesn't feel good either." Kaj moaned and slowly sat up. "Gabe took a bite out of me."

He and Oko shared a look, and images of Mooki, Gabe, Boj and Salli raced each other around and around in Kaj's mind. He knew what Oko was thinking. The same thing he was. If he died, was he going to become one of those things? Fear welled up inside him, he felt it clawing at his brain, digging into it and threatening to take him over. Instead, he took a deep breath. "I'm not dead yet Oko, I think it will take more than this to take me out."

"Of course it will." Oko didn't sound confident, but Kaj wasn't going to think about that right now. He was going to think about the people back in Munchkinville who needed him. He couldn't let them down.

Walking was more difficult that it had been before, even with Oko there to lean on. Not only did his leg hurt more, but his fingers trembled and his knees didn't feel like they could be trusted to keep him upright. Abandoned by the rush his fear had brought, each step was motivated by hunger and pure willpower.

Then he saw them, lying by the side of the road, two apples. He couldn't think of a time when something to eat had ever looked so good. Staggering toward them, he snatched one up, cupped it in both hands and devoured it. Skin, flesh and seeds alike all got shoved into his mouth and ground up into a pulpy mess. Juices ran down his chin and he swept his tongue in a wide circle to try and lap them up again. Oko chewed on the other one, though with less enthusiasm. When Kaj was left with only the apple core, he looked at it, considering.

Something out of the corner of his eye caught his attention; another apple. It lay on the ground beside an oil-stained tree stump. Tossing the core over his shoulder, he picked up the second apple. It was badly damaged, as though it had been thrown with great force toward the ground, but it looked far more appetizing than the apple core had.

Kaj ate the second apple as they continued on their way down the Yellow Brick Road. He was putting more weight on Oko than he had been earlier in the day, but he counted each step forward as a victory.

It was difficult to keep up his pace though, his leg hurt. It hurt a lot. He could feel heat emanating off it if he held his hand close, and the edges that had once been red were darkening, turning almost black. What's more, the red line was climbing further and further up his leg. It now disappeared somewhere under the hem of his knee-length shorts. Bending his leg become painful as well, so he'd taken to leaving it straight and dragging it along behind him. That method of walking meant he made progress, but it wasn't doing his shoes any good and it was definitely slowing him down.

Oko hadn't said anything more about his injury, but more than once Kaj caught him looking at it worriedly, his thoughts written plainly across his face. Kaj had turned away when he'd seen that. His own fear was barely contained, he didn't want Oko's to turn it loose.

The sun was at its highest point when they came to the woods. "You know, my mom always told me scary stories about the lions, tigers and bears that are supposed to live in the forest."

"Mine too," Oko replied. "But they just aren't scary compared to...well, you know."

"Yeah, I know." Kaj replied and entered the forest beside Oko without hesitation.

After a time, the lengthening shadows told him the sun was getting lower but he kept going, determined not to stop until he saw the walls of the Emerald City. Visions of the munchkins back home who relied on him danced through his mind, coupled with the memory of him telling Mooki "I don't know, why don't you go find out?".

"I told Mooki to check out what was in the house," he blurted, his voice as parched as his throat.

Oko stopped and turned to look at him. "You did what?"

"I...well, I tried to stop him afterward, but...I mean, I thought it was just a cat..." his words trailed off weakly.

"You couldn't have known," Oko said, patting his shoulder and shifting so that Kaj could use him for support once more. "You couldn't have known."

Kaj swallowed back tears and kept going, trying to think about anything to take his mind off what might be going on back home and the pain in his calf.

His leg felt different. They paused for a moment so he could assess it. Heat continued to come off it in waves, the edges were black and the center was olive with pus, but the pain was different. The wound itself no longer hurt, but the rest of his calf did. His entire leg was swollen so much he feared his skin might split, and when he lifted his shirt to check he could see the red line climbing from his leg toward his chest.

"I can leave you here, and come back for you," Oko suggested, looking at the mess on his calf.

The idea was tempting. He could just rest. Sit down at the base of one of these trees, relax and sleep. Sleep sounded wonderful. But he couldn't. He knew the pictures in his head wouldn't stop until he sent help back to Munchkinville. He felt responsible. He'd sent Mooki into the house and then led him right back to Boj's house. He had to be a part of the end of this. He had to get to Emerald City.

He shook his head. "No, I can go on." His voice didn't sound like his own. It was dry and rough. He was thirstier than he'd ever been in his life, with no water in sight. Still, he had to go on.

Kaj limped along the Yellow Brick Road, whose edges blurred and swayed in his eyes, dragging his leg along with him and holding on tight to Oko. When they left the forest he could see Emerald City shimmering in front of him and briefly felt his knees sag with relief.

I must be hallucinating, Kaj thought. The only thing between them and Emerald City was a poppy field. It stretched as far as he could see to both the left and right, but its scarlet flowers were all dusted with snow. Snow, in the middle of summer. They paused by the entrance of the field and he grabbed a handful of snow, held it over his open mouth and squeezed, but instead of the cold trickle of water he'd expected he got nothing. Nothing. The snow stuck together but didn't melt. He breathed on it. Still nothing. He crammed it into his mouth, but it tasted like sand so he spat it out. Some sort of magic kept it cold, and kept him from being able to drink.

He stepped with his left foot and dragged his right. Brick by brick down the road with Oko supporting most of his weight for him. The whole while Kaj's voice chanted in his mind, one syllable with each step. Water. Glinda. Water. Glinda. Left. Right. Left. Right.

The city glistened in front of him, a myriad of shades of green, but Kaj was in no shape to admire it. All he wanted now was to get to the city, to help and water.

His leg hurt with every step. Not a dull throbbing pain, but a sharp ache that reverberated through his entire body and made him cry out more than once.

Still, he kept going. Wa. Left. Ter. Right. Glin. Left. Da. Right.

"You can do this," Oko said. All Kaj could do was nod.

Finally they reached the gate. He'd expected it to be guarded but it wasn't. In fact, he didn't see anyone anywhere. He heard them though.

Voices lifted in celebration came to him from down the street. He heard cheering, laughter and several different songs being sung simultaneously and moved, toward the sound.

A flash of color overhead caught Kaj's eye, and he stopped to gaze up at the odd thing. A giant balloon with the words "OMAHA STATE FAIR" emblazoned on it soared overhead. A big wooden basket containing a man hung beneath it.

Certain his fever had overcome him, Kaj shook his head to clear the bizarre vision, but it persisted and he watched as the silent balloon lifted further up into the air, growing smaller and smaller.

A terrible pain clutched his chest, like a fist grabbing him around his ribs and squeezing with all its might. Kaj gasped, struggling to suck in air and stay on his feet as the pain pulsed there and refused to let go. He stumbled and would have fallen to his knees if not for Oko's strong arm around him. Waves of heat washed through him, as they pushed through noisy crowd. Glinda would help him, he thought. He was hurt and thirsty.

Turning a corner he saw a forest of bodies. Munchkins and Quadlings and Gilikins all standing together, shoulder to shoulder in front of him. The crowd had stopped cheering, but a low murmuring sound emanated from it, and over the hum, a familiar voice. Wait, Kaj thought through the fog of pain enveloping him. Two familiar voices.

"Then close your eyes," he heard Glinda say, her voice dripping with honey, "and tap your heels together three times. And think to yourself, there's no place like home."

"There she is!" Oko shouted, and began to use push people out of his way as he rushed toward the stage, with Kaj in tow.

Dorothy's voice came to him, soft as a whisper, or a dream. "There's no place like home," she said. He felt the grip on his chest tighten once more and moaned in pain. In front of him he saw Glinda's face, then his gaze dropped to her throat, to the pulse beating there. He imagined all the wet blood beneath her skin. Just there, so close. So wet.

"There's no place like home," Dorothy repeated, and Kaj, filled with a burst of strength, wrenched himself from Oko's grip and lunged for Glinda's throat. If he could only have a little drink. Just a little. Enough to ease his parched throat, to soothe his pain...

"There's no place like home," Dorothy said one last time, just as Kaj bit down.

That's when the screaming started.

Like a magpie, **Rhonda Parrish** is constantly distracted by shiny things. She's the editor of many anthologies and author of plenty of books, stories and poems. She lives with her husband and three cats in Edmonton, Alberta, and she can often be found there playing Dungeons and Dragons, bingeing crime dramas or cheering on the Oilers.

Her website, updated regularly, is at http://www.rhondaparrish.com and her Patreon, updated even more regularly, is at https://www.patreon.com/RhondaParrish.

If you enjoy this book please consider supporting my Patreon where, for as little as $1 a month you get:

- **Exclusive stories and poems you can't read anywhere else**

- **Behind-the-scenes access to make sure you are always 100% in the loop**

- **Early access to books, stories, cover reveals and inside information**

- **Books, stories and merch in your inbox and your mailbox**

And more!

<u>Click here to access and for more information</u>
(or copy/paste this into your browser →
https://www.patreon.com/RhondaParrish)

Always Be The First To Know!

Whether it's a new release, a call for submissions, cover reveal, super sale or I just want to share a new story I've written, you will always be among the first to know if you sign up for my newsletter.

I promise to respect your privacy and your inbox. I will only email you when I have something exciting to share, probably about twice a month.

Subscribe now and you'll receive a free download of my award-winning post-apocalyptic short story, "Starry Night" as a welcome-to-the-newsletter present!

Subscribe to Rhonda's Mailing List!

http://bit.ly/StarryStory

ALSO BY RHONDA PARRISH

APHANASIAN STORIES

WASTE NOT (AND OTHER FUNNY ZOMBIE STORIES)
WHITE NOISE: POETRY OF THE ZOMBIE APOCALYPSE
THE OTHER SIDE OF THE DOOR

HOLLOW

EERIE EDMONTON
HAUNTED HOSPITALS

RHONDA PARRISH ANTHOLOGIES

Available Now

A IS FOR APOCALYPSE
B IS FOR BROKEN
C IS FOR CHIMERA
D IS FOR DINOSAUR
E IS FOR EVIL
F IS FOR FAIRY

FAE
CORVIDAE
SCARECROW
SIRENS
EQUUS

MRS. CLAUS: NOT THE FAIRY TALE THEY SAY
TESSERACTS TWENTY-ONE: NEVERTHELESS
METASTASIS
NITEBLADE MAGAZINE

FIRE: DEMONS, DRAGONS AND DJINNS
EARTH: GIANTS, GOLEMS AND GARGOYLES
AIR: SYLPHS, SPIRITS AND SWAN MAIDENS

GRIMM, GRIT AND GASOLINE
CLOCKWORK, CURSES AND COAL

HEAR ME ROAR

SWASHBUCKLING CATS: NINE LIVES ON THE SEVEN SEAS